ISBN: 9798874112363
ASIN:B0CMFDRB46
Imprint: Independently published

1

The Lost Omega
By
Laura Rush

Book 1
Into the Woods Trilogy

DEDICATION:

**"The devil whispered into my ear:
'You're not strong enough to withstand the
storm.'
I whispered back:
'I am the storm.' – Adharanand Finn**

*For the ones fighting a battle no one else knows
about.*

PLAYLIST

Rescue – Lauren Daigle
Birthday cake (his version) – Dylan Conrique
Control – Zoe Wees
Not us – Loving Caliber
Running with the wolves – Aurora
Wolves – Sam Tinnesz
Youth – Daughter
May I have this dance – Meadowlark
Never let me go – Florence + The Machine
Sleeping on the blacktop – Colter Wall
Clean – Taylor Swift

TRIGGER WARNING LIST

CONTENTS

Copyright

Playlist & Trigger warnings

Wolf terminology

Prologue

Chapter 1 – Elara

Chapter 2 – Alpha Asher

Chapter 3 – Elara

Chapter 4 - Alpha Asher

Chapter 5 – Elara

Chapter 6 - Alpha Asher

Chapter 7 – Elara

Chapter 8 - Lola

Chapter 9 – Kylo

Chapter 10 - Elara

Chapter 11 - Alpha Asher

Chapter 12 - Elara

Chapter 13 - Alpha Asher

Chapter 14 - Elara

Chapter 15 - Alpha Asher

Acknowledgements

About the author

WOLF TERMINOLOGY

Alpha – leader of the pack, usually the strongest, the largest wolf in the pack. He's the protecter, the decision maker of all he leads.

Beta –second in command, Alpha's right-hand man/ bestie.

Luna –Alpha's fated mate, seen as mother to all in the pack.

Omega –lowest rank member in the pack, usually treated poorly and as a house maid/servant.

Moon Goddess –the creator of the wolves.

Pack warrior/ hunter –the strongest members after the alpha. Basically, the pack's army.

Mate / fated mate – a wolf's soulmate, their other half in life. Wolves are with their fated mate or with no one. They can only meet their fated mate after the first shift or when they turn the age of eighteen.

Pup/Pupling- young wolf who has yet to shift or meet their inner wolf.

Rogues –belong to no pack. Free and wild. These wolves can be seen as dangerous, but this is only a small group.

Shifting / shift –shifting from human form into the wolf form

Your Wolf / inner wolf – once you have completed the first shift, you unlock your wolf, which has a fully functioning brain, and as you are connected as one body… you can talk to them in your head, they are like an annoying song you cannot get out your head.

Mindlink / link – the ability to talk with another wolf without speaking aloud. Pack members can only mindlink other members in the same pack.

Pack house – think huge house—where the best wolves live. (Alpha, beta, luna, warriors, etc)

Vampire – immortal, invisible, dislikes the sun, sharp teeth, love sucking your blood, allergy to garlic.

Witch / the coven – puts spells on you. Warts. Spell books. Speak in another language.

Elders –the oldest member of the pack, usually the most knowledgeable.

Werewolf council – They are the law in the wolf world.

Heat –a period for shewolves but only stronger, more painful with an increased sex drive that gets more intense with each passing day.

Wolfsbane –kills wolves. Usually found on knifes or bullets.

Rejected – when a big bad mean wolf does not like his/her fated mate he/she rejects the soulmate, causing them absolute agony and a broken heart. In some cases, wolves have died from rejection.

Hybrid - a cross between a wolf, human, and either a witch or vampire.

PROLOGUE

THE TALE OF THE ELEMENTS.

Thousands of years ago, two Moon Goddesses, Diana, and Hecate—sisters by blood—were given their own moons and elements.

Both sisters were graced with the ability to create life.

Hecate—Goddess of the Dark Moon and Underworld, was gifted the elements of fire, spirit, and air.

Diana—Goddess of the Full Moon, was given the elements of earth and water.

For many of years, they lived in harmony. Diana, who loved all and was loved by all, wanted to bless earth with love and hope, so she created wolves. Not ordinary wolves, no, she gave them the abilities of strength, power, and heightened senses, who could shift between human and wolf.

Each born wolf was presented with an element of earth or water. The earth element allowed her wolves to protect, heal, and shield, while the water element allowed them to adapt in any environment on land or in sea. She gave them the ability find a fated mate, she ensured all wolves had a one true love. There was no hierarchy, just packs and each pack lived in peace.

Hecate, on the other hand, preferred order. So, she created the coven of three sisters: Maya, Isabella, and Jasmine. She gave them her elements of spirit and air, which allowed them to time travel, create magic, and transform weather patterns.

However, Hecate was not satisfied with this; she wanted more, a one true leader of all. One who would stand above all life forms. One with all elements of power.

On one dark winter's evening, Hecate had travelled to earth and found a human boy. She had her coven perform magic for weeks, and the boy was tortured, chained, and poisoned... Until, one day, he fought back.

Using his own dark magic, he surpassed the sisters, and Hecate declared him her king. The boy, Ozul, became known as the vampire king. Hecate blessed him with the element of fire, protecting him with invisibility and immortality.

Diana was unaware of Hecate's dark nature.

Hecate had begged her sister to band together and give Ozul all elements. Diana disagreed. She believed it to be wrong and argued that the gods who gave them their elements would have created this being, should it have been the way.

Hecate grew impatient and devised a plan with Ozul and the coven. Between the five of them, they created a large army of witches and vampires to overthrow Diana and the wolves.

A long time had passed since Diana had seen or spoken with Hecate.

Diana became weaker and weaker as her wolves destroyed each other for blood. Packs were outraged that wolves where being kidnapped from their borders. They believed it to be their own mistreating each other for power. No pack felt safe, and each slowly declared war or retreated into hiding.

It soon became apparent to Diana that something more sinister was happening in the shadows, Ozul and his vampires joined the pack war and quickly the wolves were dying out.

As Diana believed it to be over, she visited a young wolf named Gundolf, gave him the title of Alpha King, and passed over the last of her powers to him, making him the strongest largest white wolf in history.

He led his pack with fierceness and great force, turning them into an army. After recruiting other packs to join his cause, he slowly but surely started to overturn the vampires and witches.

This continued for many centuries until Gundolf's great, great grandson Elrick declared the vampires and witches were no more.

Hecate, the vampire king, and the coven were never seen again. It was said they had retreated to the underworld.

Diana had visited Elrick many of times in his dreams but was never seen in person.

A treaty of reconciliation was formed amongst all packs' Alphas, and each were to go back to their homelands and live in peace.

ΔΔΔ

CHAPTER 1 – ELARA

7 years ago, 11 years old

I fall to the ground, screaming until the whole room falls still. I feel like I've been thrown into the darkest corners of hell, as hot streams of tears fall down my face. Voices are calling my name, but they're low and distant. The pain in my chest is too much to bear.

Their gone, their gone—my parents are dead. I'm all alone.

June 14th – 2 years ago, 16 years old

"You're a filthy little mutt," Maddox Addison sneers through gritted teeth as he kicks me repeatedly in my stomach. "You don't belong here; I should just kill you now and be done with you."

I lay still, taking the blows, refusing to give Maddox any indication of the pain I am in. I have learned if I don't respond, the beating is less severe.

It's been this way since Alpha Blake Addison, the leader of the Shadow Shifters Pack, broke the news that my parents had been killed in a freak car accident on the way home from a treaty meeting with other pack leaders. He moved me out of my family home, the one I had spent my entire life in, and placed me into the pack orphanage.

"Elara, your parents' death is a tragic loss to us all. Your father was my best friend and go-to person. I will miss him dearly, as will the entire pack. I cannot imagine the pain you are in. Which is why I think it's best if you're around children your age who have also lost loved ones, people who know what you have been through and are going to go through. This might help you grieve and move on. We are all here to help and support you. You're still a highly valued and loved member of this pack."

Over the first year of losing my parents, I lost count of how many times I went to Alpha Blake to tell him how I was being treated by Maddox and his gang, and each time, he had a reason or excuse. *"Elara, sweetheart, I know you're struggling. I'm here to support you. I'm sure Maddox didn't mean it. He's a good wolf."*

I once showed him the bruising to my ribs and body, and he just dismissed me with a stern look.

I'm not sure if the reason I stopped going to him was the realisation Maddox is his son, the next in line after him to become the leader of the pack. He's not going to help me over him or if it was me accepting this is my life now. With no family, I became the lowest rank member, an Omega. The stories I had been told growing up were how omegas were slaves, easily disposed of, so it doesn't matter what the future holds, I will always be trash to this pack.

Present day – June 14th – 18 years old

I blow out the candle on my cupcake one of the other orphans, Lola, aka my best friend, had placed on my bedside table this morning. "Happy birthday to me," I mutter to myself, then exhale a shaky breath.

After crawling out from underneath my blanket, I place my feet on the cold tile and pad over to the window. Usually, everyone would be going about their normal daily routine: the youngling pups being walked to school, the enforcers doing perimeter checks, and the shops opening. This morning is different, though, not because it's my birthday, but because the mating ceremony is being held at our pack house.

My pack sits in the woods, miles from humans so one doesn't stumble into our territory but close enough for us to get to anything we need anything that our camp doesn't have. It really is a beautiful place. The forest encompasses the hundreds of cabins which house the pack's families. Some line the long path to the Pack House where Alpha Blake, his fated mate—our luna—and Maddox live, along with our beta and his family. We also have a pack school and medical center.

A loud bang goes off behind me, interrupting my thoughts. Lola and a pup come rushing into my bedroom, nearly taking my door off its hinges. "Happy birthday to you, happy birthday to Elara, happy birthday to you. Hooray," they sing at the top of their lungs, smiling from ear to ear.

"Thanks, guys." I muster my best smile and give them each a hug.

"We sang it, now scram, pup. I need to talk to Elara," Lola says to Jack as she pats him on his head, then he turns to me, smiles, diving back into my arms and waves before heading back through the door.

Jack's my little pup, when he arrived here at the orphanage, at only three years old, he had no one, I can remember Alpha Blake just dropping his bag on the floor and pushing his back to urge him to come into the building. He cried for hours, I could not take seeing him like that, I hugged him so tight, whispering promises that it was all going to be okay. He slept in my bed that night, from then on, he became my shadow, following me around were ever I went. Lola took on the big sister role while I took on more of a mother's role. I like to make sure he knows how loved he is, that he is never alone, he will *always* have me.

Lola skips over to me and swoops me into a big embrace. "Happy birthday, babe, you're finally eighteen! This is the age we've been waiting for!"

The age all wolves look forward to—when we meet our wolf and shift for the first time. Your wolf is your other half, not like our fated mates, but our wolf gives us the ability to have increased senses, strength, speed, and reflexes. Being connected to our wolf allows us to mindlink with them. They say your wolf will appear once you've had your first shift. Luckily, I don't have to wait too long for that to happen, as your first shift happens on the full moon following your eighteenth birthday, and the next is in three days.

Eighteen is also the age we can meet our fated mate given to us by our moon goddess. We grew up being told tale after tale of fated mates. Fated mates are said to be the other half of your soul, which means that when you are bound together, you become one. They say when you meet your fated mate the connection snaps into place instantly and the bond is formed. Your fated mate is your lover, protector, from that day on.

"My fated mate could reject me, I am an omega the lowest one in the pack, who wants to have that as a mate?"I groan, slumping back down to sit on the side of my bed. "And even if he accepts me, I might be worse off than I am here. You know how male wolves treat omegas, they are just punching bags and meal getters. And what about Jack? What will happen then I promised id never to leave him" I sigh.

"Then first off, he'd be one stupid fucking wolf, and second Jack will have me if you're not here."

That makes me smile. She's had my back since I arrived here seven years ago. Lola is eighteen too; her birthday was two weeks ago. She's a small and petite, almost pixie looking with her short dark hair, brown doe eyes, and freckles. Her mom died during childbirth, and she never knew her dad, so Alpha Blake placed her here to "*be with kids like herself.*" *Urgggh.*

Lola continues, "Plus, if the tales are true, he'd die from heartbreak if he rejected you!" She sits down next to me and wraps her arm around my shoulder, trying to comfort me.

"We don't know if that's true, Lo,"I whisper. I used to be excited waiting for the day I come of age and get my wolf, the day I get my chance to have a love like Mom and Dad's, but now it makes me feel sick.

All wolves over the age of eighteen may attend the mating ceremony despite rank in the pack, and each pack takes turns holding a mating ceremony. Like is said, this morning is different - In four days, hundreds of eligible wolves from different packs will travel to our territory hoping to meet their fated mate.

But for me, the chance of rejection looming has me anxious. *I need to get out of here with Jack before then... Somehow...*

One thing I could thank Alpha Blake for, is allowing me to have access to my inheritance before I came of age. Although I live in an orphanage, I've had money in my pocket, and it's given me hope in my darkest moments knowing I could escape and survive outside the pack. I've barely spent any of it. Not that I've had chance to; most days I'm working wherever the enforcers tell me to.

Today, I'm cleaning out the grand hall in the pack house in preparation for tomorrow.

"Oh, look what the dirt dragged in." Maddox slithers up behind me as I polish the floor on my hands and knees. "While you're down there, mutt." As I turn to face him, he pulls his penis out and swings it in front of me.

Maddox is a handsome man, with brown hair that flows to his shoulders, ocean-blue eyes, a chiselled jaw line, and bulky muscles. A deep v sculpts his stomach, which flexes as he walks. I don't think he owns a shirt, at least I have never seen him wear one. The worst thing is he knows he looks good. He's cocky and arrogant. A fucking pig.

I say nothing and go back to shining the marbled flooring. "Such a shame a pretty face like yours is wasted."

Before I can tell him to leave me alone and go away, he grips me by my hair and yanks me up off the floor before slamming me back down to my knees. His teeth are bared as he grits out, "Open your fucking mouth, bitch!"

My eyes are wide with fear, and I'm sure he can hear my heart thumping out of my chest. I glance around to see if there is anyone watching, but mysteriously, they have all disappeared. I croak out,"No."

Maddox gives me an evil smile and forces his dick into my mouth. His girth stretches my lips, and the tip of his dick hits my throat, causing me to choke. Tears stream down my face as he wraps my hair tighter around his hand, making me fear I'll find a bald patch there later. "Eyes on me, mutt,"he snarls.

I know how this goes. It isn't my first rodeo with him taking whatever he wants from me, so I glare up at him, hoping he can see the hatred in my eyes. Something tells me he might get a thrill from that, though.

"Grab my fucking ass and force me into your mouth, now,"he demands. I do as I'm told, digging my nails into his ass, and forcing him down my throat while silently praying to the moon goddess to fire a lightning bolt up his ass so I can run and get out of here as fast as I can.

Maddox moans, letting me know he is close to finishing. "You're such a pretty little slut."He groans as his hot, salty release squirts across my tongue, then I gag and force myself to swallow it down. His eyes are glazed over until he roars out a laugh and releases my hair. While pulling his dick from my mouth and tucking himself away, he stares into my eyes, then I put my head down to wait for him to leave.

Grabbing my chin, he forces me to look at him, and he says, "I hope your first shift kills you tonight, and if it doesn't, just don't get your hopes up for tomorrow, mutt, the moon goddess isn't stupid enough to give you a fated mate."He turns and walks out of the hall without another word.

Ouch. What if he's right? The moon goddess didn't save my parents, so why would she give me a fated mate? I need to leave tonight after I shift. It's too risky to stay.

I'm becoming a rogue wolf.

CHAPTER 2 – ALPHA ASHER

June 17th – 1 day before the mating ceremony

"Asher, we are all set to go. Should take us about five hours," my beta and best friend, Kylo, informs me as he strolls into my office. I sense he's on edge about the ceremony. He's second in command, and if all goes wrong tomorrow, he'll be left to lead the pack.

It's been a decade since any of us have been to a mating ceremony, as we were cast out by the werewolf council ten years ago. War had been sparked by some of the other packs wanting to take control of every pack, and my father, the alpha before me, took it upon himself to make The Blood Moon Pack, the peacekeeper group. However, when our pack turned up at the war zone, others turned on us, and we had to defend ourselves. We were the strongest by a long shot and slaughtered three packs in minutes.

We were a threat to all, so they banished us.

"We must try, Kylo, if they won't accept us via other forms of communication, then they can at least hear us out face-to-face. The mating-ceremony laws state no packs can attack. It's open to any wolf eligible to find a mate. I've scrolled through every text to hand nothing is stopping us,"I say, trying to keep a calm, soothing voice to ease his worry.

He sighs and flops down into my office chair. "Yeah, I know, you said this already, but I still think it's a bad idea, as do other pack members. What if they turn on us? We will be outnumbered."

I've thought this through for a long time, and we have no other choice. Without the ability to meet our fated mates, our pack line is dying out, and only your fated mate can give you a pup. Some of the pack members have tried during heat season when female wolves are most fertile to impregnate and carry our pack on but have had no success. We have few pups among us and that's solely down to luck that a few pack members have met their fated mate in our pack.

"I will talk to the pack before we leave, settle any concerns."I exhale."It's our only option."I'm not sure who I'm trying to convince more, myself or Kylo.

△△△

"Hey, we ready to get this shitshow over with?"Kylo shouts from behind the car after loading the last of our bags into the trunk.

"Yeah, just give me ten minutes to speak with Ella, I won't be long." I make my way back into the pack house and up the staircase in search of my sister. Ella is hard to track down; if she doesn't want to talk or be around anyone, she tends to disappear, and sometimes it's like she's invisible. Ella is ten years younger than me. I figured a long while ago the way she is down to our parent's dying when she was only eight years old.

It wasn't until she turned ten that I noticed there was more going on than just a grieving preadolescent pup. She wouldn't sleep at night, but she slept all day and barely functioned or ate.

I had worried for months until she awakened me in the early hours, screaming, "Asher, wake up, wake up." Her tiny body shook, and her heart raced.

"Ella, what's wrong?" I'd attempted to sooth her by placing my hands on her shoulders.

"Rogues—" She panted. "Coming. They are coming, Asher," she cried.

"How do you know?" I asked while mindlinking Kylo to run a perimeter check.

"It's hard to explain, but for now, you need to get extra warriors on the east side of the pack, and quick." She ran out of the room.

Before I could chase her down, Kylo screamed *"Rogue attack, east side*!" through our mindlink. *What the fuck?!* I shook myself from my thoughts. How Ella knew they were on route would have to wait, I had a pack to protect. Jumping up from my bed onto my feet, I called my wolf forward, allowing him to take over. "*You know what to do,*" I told him.

"*Leave the fuckers to me,*" he had growled.

Coming out of my flashback, I was left with the one thought: That morning changed the fate of our pack forever. With Ella informing us rogues were coming, we were able to fight them off and keep them from coming into the village. Without Ella's alert, we would have been caught off guard and outnumbered. It would have been the bloodiest day in pack history. Maybe even the last.

△△△

"Ella," I call out as I enter her room.

"You're still going, then, I guess?" Disapproval dripped from each word, and she's still hidden from view.

"Yes, El, I need to do this, you know why." I sniff her scent out and drop down onto all fours and peep under her bed. "Please come out from under there." I'm trying to keep my facial expression neutral and warm because if I show her a tiny ounce of the nerves I'm feeling about this trip, it will send her spiralling. That's the last thing I need to deal with. She stares into my eyes for a moment before nodding and rolling out from under her bed.

As I'm getting back onto my feet her soft voice comes through my mind. "*You know this is a bad idea, right, Ash? I understand you're alpha and the*

pack needs you, but there must be another way."
Ella's voice cracks, and my heart pangs.

I'm unsure how I can reassure her when our parents died because they had tried to do what I would do tomorrow at the mating ceremony. They went to plead our pack's innocence and good nature to prove we were no threat to them. Unfortunately, they were brutally murdered by Alpha Blake Addison. The exact person I need to not murder at the ceremony and need to convince to let me onto his pack lands to speak with the werewolf council. I can see why my pack, Kylo, and Ella are worried. But with my parents' passing, came the law that no packs can fight during the mating ceremony, so I have hope the packs will obey and let us in, with zero bloodshed.

This is our only way for survival.

△△△

CHAPTER 3 – ELARA

The first shift is said to be ruthlessly painful, each bone snapping, bending, and growing, then sprouting hairs to form your wolf. My parents met in the pack and were the same age and best friends since they were pups. They always told me how they believed they had the easiest shift, and they knew they were fated mates even before they found out the moon goddess has granted them that wish. Shifting on the same full moon, side by side, they comforted each other while others around them howled and screamed in pain. Mom said it was because your mate can ease pain.

Most first-time shifters brought family members to stand with them during the process to talk them through it, and the rest of pack could watch from afar, but since I'm an omega orphan, I was never allowed to. Sometimes, we could hear the screams from the orphanage if we sat on the front steps, but none of us have witnessed one.

I have no family left to be with me tonight, but I'm thankful I have Lola, who is also doing her first shift. Hopefully, they place us together, and we can help each other through it.

Nerves swirl at what feels like hundred miles per hour in my stomach, and my hands shake in front of me as I attempt to slow my heartbeat.

"Elara, you ready?" Lola asks from my bedroom door.

Taking a few more deep breaths and slowly exhaling, I turn to face her. She's wearing her favourite outfit: an electric-blue corset top and tight black leather pants and boots. I smile at her.

"You know you're gonna shred those clothes to pieces when you shift, right?"

I let out a chuckle at the end and point to her clothes.

Lola shrugs, then walks into my room, and stands in front of me. "Nah, I won't. I'll just get butt naked before it starts, and then no clothes will be ruined, problem solved." We laugh. I have always admired her honesty and no-shit-taking attitude. It's probably why Maddox and his trolls don't go after her.

"Hey, I'm gonna be right there with you, okay? You're not alone." Tears stream down my face, and I launch myself into her arms and squeeze her.

"I know," I whisper. "Everything's going to change now, and I'd be lying if I said I was ready for any of it." Lola sniffles, then hugs me tighter. If she knew I planned to leave after tonight's shift, not only would she flip out, but she would also demand to join me. I can't bring her or Jack, though. It's too risky; it's going to break my heart but who knows what's going to happen once I cross the border.

Lola pulls herself together, then shakes her arms out. Looking into my eyes with determination, she replies, "Damn straight it's gonna change, but this time, for the better, I know it." She says it with so much confidence, I wish I could muster as much as her in this moment, and then I know I would make it through.

If I speak, I might crumble, so I nod toward the door, and she returns the nod and grabs my hand, pulling me out the door and to the training field where the shifting takes place.

△△△

"Try and stay by my side," I say to Lola as we reach the edge of the field.

She squeezes my hand and turns her head toward me, smiling. "Always, babe."

"Aw, look, guys, it's some of the orphan brigade, where's your mommy's and daddy's, hey?" He mocks with a sly smile creeping across his face.

"Ah, if it isn't diddy dick Dylan," Lola replies, stopping in front of him. "Did Tracy manage to find it this time?" She turns to me and winks.

"Whatever she said, it's not true," he grits out, his arms sprouting hairs.

"T-N-M-P, dude." Lola flips him the bird, then stops to inspect her nails.

"What the fuck does that even mean, weirdo?" he snaps.

She rolls her eyes and shakes her head. "It means totally not my problem, fucktard." As she turns her back, he launches forward but is pulled by his collar by Alpha Blake, who looks toward Lola and back to him.

"I understand your nerves are high, but let's all try and stay calm. Remember, we are all family here." He looks at me as he says "family." A sense of courage rises inside me, but before I can ask him to define the word family, Maddox strolls through the training field with a swagger to his step. I bite my lip and look down at the ground.

"Let's have all first-time shifters in the centre of the field, please," Alpha Blake yells. Lola grabs my arm and drags me to the centre. I turn around to glance at the crowd of watchers behind us. When I meet Maddox's eyes, I stop, and he gives me a sly grin and grabs his crotch before arching a brow at me. I whirl around and clench my fists at my sides. Please, goddess, please, let me have a wolf.

Lola whispers, "Please, moon goddess, don't let him be either of our mates." I flick my gaze in her direction and she's looking at Maddox. Fear rises inside me, and my vision goes blurry as Alpha Blake begins his speech.

Bile rises to my throat as the horrible thoughts take over. What if Maddox is my mate? He never found his when he turned eighteen, and I know he's been looking for her. Everyone in the pack knows you're a stronger alpha with your mate by your side, and everyone knows this is why Alpha Blake hasn't stepped down yet. He apparently made a promise to hand over his title to Maddox once he found his fated mate. Please, goddess, don't let it be me.

I'm pulled out of my worst-nightmare thoughts when a blood curdling scream comes from beside me. Lola is on her knees, holding her stomach, butt naked with her clothes in a neat pile beside her. She launches herself forward and is on all fours when her back arches and her bones snap. I try soothing her, but it doesn't work. A group of guys laughs behind us, mimicking a doggy-style position with each other and pointing at Lola.

With anger pushing me back to my feet, I make my way over to them, ready to give them a piece of my mind. As I step forward, the ground spins and a sharp pain in my back drops me to my knees. I scream and look down to my hands as claws push from my fingertips. The pain increases, and I cry out as hair spreads across my arms and legs. My yellow dress rips as my bones snap. Maddox storms toward me, but I'm in too much pain to care about what he wants now. My arms snap, and before I can face-plant, Maddox grip my shoulders.

"You're nearly done, the first shift is always the worst. After this, it will get easier." His voice is soft and almost caring. I snarl at him, and he smiles.

"That's the spirit." He laughs. Jumping back, I close my eyes, and when my last bone breaks, I huff out a sigh.

Gasps come from the crowd, and I open my eyes to the pack members gawking at me open-mouthed. Maddox stares up at me with furrowed brows. Alpha Blake stands next to him and calls for the pack elders. I forget I'm in wolf form and try to talk, but a howl comes out instead, making everyone around me jump.

Thoughts race through my mind. and a wet nose rubs against my legs. A brown wolf, half my size with dark-hazel eyes, looks up at me.

"Elara." Alpha Blake's voice comes through mind.

I look down at him and tilt my head. *"Yes, Alpha?"*

"That's Lola beside you." I look back down at the wolf and lick her head, then she flops out her tongue and nips at my legs.

I yelp before turning back to Alpha Blake. *"Why is everyone so small and looking at me funny?"*

He gives me a small smile. *"We can discuss that later, but right now, I need you to shift back and go to office. I will join you shortly,"* he commands, keeping me from asking why I can't join the first run by shutting off our link. Then he announces to the crowd that the first run of the night is about to take place. He shifts, jumping into the air in human form and landing on all fours in wolf form in one swift motion.

His deep-black fur matches his eyes, and only an alpha wolf should be as big as he is, yet I, an omega, stand as tall as him. Dropping my snout, I'm taken aback by the bright-white shade of my fur. I've never seen a white wolf before.

What am I?

CHAPTER 4 – ALPHA ASHER

The night before the mating ceremony

We abandoned our vehicles a few hours ago, taking the rest of our journey to the Shadow shifter Pack by foot. Only carrying our backpacks with the essentials: food, water, and clothes. This way, if we need to shift into wolf form, we can carry the bags in our mouths. I figure we will be less of a target since other packs travelling won't stop for wolves, but they would notice six cars coming down dirt roads.

We watch from afar in wolf form as the Shadow Shifters Pack does their first shifter run along their pack borders. It's a full moon tonight, so you can tell it's the new shifters, as they tend to lag behind the experienced runners.

Alpha Blake and Maddox lead the front of the pack—both large wolves with black fur. Only Alpha wolves get black fur from the moon goddess.

"Now is our chance, Boss," Kylo says.

I signal to him with a nod to take a few warriors with him to check how tight their borders are. My plan is simple: Wait until Blake and his son are away from the pack, knowing they will be heavily guarded—Blake won't want to take any chances on his life being taken before the big day. Once we have a way, we can get onto the grounds without being spotted, we can bunker down for the night, then any sign of danger we can run out of here.

The team of men I brought along with Kylo and myself are our best warriors, hunters, and runners. They all know the plan. We don't attack unless we are attacked. We look out for each other, and if you're feeling in danger, you shout it through mindlink. Simple.

△△△

"Only you can fuck this up, man!" I shout to Kylo. The stupid oaf found his fated fucking mate just as they got into the borders. Not only did she scream loud enough to alert her entire pack that something was wrong, but he also chased her down farther into their territory to throw her over his shoulder and carry her back over the border.

"Dudeeeee, she's the one for me, I'm telling you," He replies.

"You're fucking joking, right? She's screaming her head off! Can't you knock her out. I don't think that's supposed to happen with your fated mate. I'm sure she's supposed to be whispering sweet nothings to you."

"Nah, she's warming up to me, I can feel it in my bones." He chuckles.

"Don't care, just shut her up and get into hiding, we're moving back to a safe place. I will alert you when it's good to come to us." I close our link off. I know he will meet up with us later. He's a big idiot, but somehow, he's a smart at the same time.

"*Men,*" I boom through my teams' links, "*We are moving back, it's no longer safe here, do not attack unless your life is threatened, got it?*" A chorus of "*Yes, Alpha*" comes from my men, and I race forward into the woods, calling them to follow me.

I saw a cave on our way in a few miles back, but my team's strong and athletic enough to get to it in no time. Hopefully, we can make it there in one piece and without being caught. If they see us before the ceremony, well, it's game over.

I cannot afford any more mistakes.

△△△

Panting from our run, we set up for the night, then gulp bottles of water. We should be fine in this cave for the night since the night chill doesn't affect us.

Even better, we made it here in one piece and without being seen. "Brock, can you get a fire going while I carry on prepping the food?" I ask.

Although I'm alpha of the pack, I don't like giving out orders while not doing anything myself. My pack will follow me wherever I go, not out of fear to obey my orders, but out of loyalty. It's my duty to protect them. My duty to look after them. A pack needs a strong leader, and I live every day of my life for each person in my pack and the future of it.

"Guess who's back?" Kylo's voice echoes around the cave. I shake my head and huff an out as the rest of the team lets out low chuckles and whistles.

"You're a fucking idiot," I mumble as he comes into view. The fire roaring behind me lets a soft glow of light show on his bulky frame and face. I wave the knife in my hand toward him and ask, "Who's the poor, unfortunate lady?" He's holding a petite girl in his arms bridal-style.

"Well truth is, we haven't exactly exchanged names yet." He smirks. "She screamed herself to sleep before she had a chance to tell me." He laughs out the last part. My men burst out laughing. All chiming in about the girl he's holding. I turn back to the ration packs I had brought in my backpack for the men and use the knife to open each one up.

Using my knife, I open each of the ration packs I brought with me while asking, "You get seen?"

"Nah, don't think so," he replies before grabbing some food packs and handing them to the men. I look behind me, and he's laid out his change of clothes on the ground and placed his mate on top of them.

"Other than screaming, did she actually say anything?" I raise a brow, then pick up the last of the food and hand it out.

As I sit down on the floor next to him, he replies, "Not really." His tone is sad, and his voice is almost a whisper. He gives me a small smile.

"Just give her some time. I mean, look at you, you scare me, fuck knows what she thought when you came creeping out of the bushes." I smirk and wink at him.

He lets out a hearty laugh. "I didn't creep out of the bushes."

"Uh, yeah you did, Beta, I was there," Reuben, a young warrior Kylo took with him on the mission, pipes up.

I laugh. "Knew it," I say while raising my hand in the air, and my men laugh.

"I bet you came out of the bushes with the dirtiest grin on your face, buck naked with your anaconda dangling between your legs, and I bet you said something along the lines of—" I clear my throat to do a deep voice impression to wind him up "My precious, my baby."

Kylo chuckles. "Not bad, but what I actually said was 'Mine.'" The men and I whistle and give him an "Ooh."

"Dickheads," he mutters.

"Actually, you said mate over and over and over again." A slow smile stretches our faces and we turn in her direction.

"'Cause that's not fucking creepy, is it?" She rolls her eyes, and I know why the moon goddess gave Kylo this girl for a fated mate. He needs someone to give him some shit and to keep his feet firmly on the ground. She crosses her arms over her chest and sits with her back against the cave wall.

"My name's Lola, and I need to go back to the pack, like right fucking now."

CHAPTER 5 – ELARA

The day of the mating ceremony

I spent all night tossing and turning.

I waited in Alpha Blake's office last night, like he asked, until someone broke through our boarders and kidnapped my best friend.

When she screamed my name, I shifted instantly, breaking the desk and doorway of Alpha Blake's office in the process. Unfortunately, the pack house guards were hot on my tail and stopped me from getting farther than the front door.

I have no idea where she is or why they took her.

Alpha Blake ordered me to the cells last night, and he said "Elara, you have me worried you will go after her, and we don't know what dangers are out there, so this is for your own safety." Funny how he didn't sound concerned and he smirked while my cell was being locked.

I feel sick, and I'm tired and uneasy. I have a terrible feeling in my gut, but I'm not sure what that is yet. My plan of escaping before the ceremony tonight has massively backfired. How the fuck am I supposed to get out of here now? Hopefully, Alpha Blake will come to his senses and let me out of here this morning. As the thought crosses my mind, footsteps come from the corridor to my left. I sit up straight. The hairs rising on my arms and back of my neck. Then his face comes into view, and I roll onto my knees as sick rises in my throat and hurl on the concrete floor.

"Eww, disgusting." He covers his mouth and nose with his hand as the smell permeates the air around us.

I wipe my mouth with my sleeve before asking, "What do you want, Maddox?"

"I've just come to let you know, white wolf." The way he says white wolf has my heart racing, and not in a safe way either. It's like he can sense my inner turmoil. "That we've decided you're going to accidently miss this year's mating ceremony." My stomach drops, my heart rate picks up, and tears well in my eyes. "Wh-what? Why, yo-yoooou can't do that." He smiles at me through the bars of the cell.

"Yes, we can, princess, yes, we fucking can. You see, your friend Lola met her fated mate last night and ran off with him and didn't even stop to think about you. She just packed her shit and left." He shrugs and waves his hand to the side.

43

No, no, she screamed for me. She wouldn't have left me without a goodbye.

I can't get my words out through the tears and Maddox's laughs.

"No one knows you're here; they think you ran off with Lola and abandoned your pack… So, you're even more disliked now, and since you're an orphan, no one's coming to save you. So yes, yes, we can do what we want with you." He turns around without another word and walks away.

I cry for what feels like forever, no one comes to give me food or a drink, and I lie on the floor looking out the small window in the cell opposite me as the daylight turns into night sky.

ΔΔΔ

"Psst, Elara, psst." I try to peel myself off the floor. My body aches as if I've been beaten. Joyful dance music plays in the distance, and I jolt up, groaning as my back pops in several places. *The mating ceremony has begun.*

I'm still half asleep when I hear my name again. "Elara" comes out on a whisper, and I look up toward the cell door. Jack is standing there.

"Jack," I whisper back while rubbing my eyes with my hands. "What are you doing here? If someone sees you—"

"No time for that, Elara, we need to hurry before someone comes, and they're all busy at the minute, but we don't have much time." His brows are furrowed, and his eyes are puffy.

"I have the keys," he whispers, "but I don't know which is the right one."

I scramble to my feet and rush to him. "It's okay, give me the keys, and you run and hide, okay?" I muster every bit of courage I can for his sake and don't show him how scared I am for him. I'm unsure what they would do if they found him here with me. He places a bundle of keys in my hand, then runs around the corner, out of sight.

With shaky hands, I place the first key into the lock and give it a wiggle, and nothing happens. Cursing, I pull the key out and put the next one in the lock and turn it, but it doesn't work. *Fuck.*

Footsteps come from the top of the corridor to my left, along with a flashlight, so I turn toward where Jack went and spot his head peering around the corner and tears coming down his face. Waving my free hand at him, I mouth, *Run* in an attempt to save him from whoever is coming.

It's now or never, I say to myself. I close my eyes and flip to the next key, trying not to clink the keys and alert whoever it is that I'm trying to break free. Putting the key in, I twist, and it clinks open. Maddox calls from the top of the corridor, "Tommy, we need you upstairs, now."

The flashlight turns off and the footsteps fade into the distance. I let out a huge breath and push open the cell door.

I round the corner, and Jack jumps up into my arms, and his little body is shaking, and small sobs come from him. "It's okay, Jack, I'm here, and I'm taking you with me."

△△△

CHAPTER 6 – ALPHA ASHER

The night of the mating ceremony

"We are not going back for some girl, Kylo," I shout at him. Turns out, his fated mate can twist the balls of my best friend pretty quickly.

"So why are we here, then? You heard Lola, they are treating their pack like slaves, so let's turn this into a rescue mission and try the fated-mates thing again next year!"

Fucking typical Kylo response.

"Okay, so we do it your girl's way, Kylo, and they notice they are missing a group of orphans, then what? All-out war is what. And that's what we are trying to avoid." I slump onto a rock and rub my temples to ease some stress.

The plan of going into the pack lands and asking for a chance is a no go. Lola laughed in my face for thirty minutes over the idea.

"Look, Lola and I can keep the pack going for a while," Kylo whispers. I side-eye him and raise a brow.

"What the fucking fuck does that mean?" Lola snaps and I smirk.

"Pups, baby, we have pups; keep the pack alive." He smiles like it's the best idea ever. I must hand it to him, he either has a death wish or genuinely thinks what he said is okay. *Your funeral, Kylo.*

"P-U-P-S?" She punctuates each letter, and the men behind her start laughing.

Kylo goes to respond, but she holds up a finger to her lips, shushing him.

"Not on your life, pal. I ain't no pup-making machine. I'm not your bitch, I'm not your slave, your mommy, your chef, or your bed warmer, got it?" then she walks away.

Kylo freezes before speaking. "She's definitely warming up to me, ain't she?"

△△△

After spending a few more hours fighting back and forth with Lola and Kylo, I concede and agree to let them and four warriors go back into the pack lands and retrieve the girl, who I've learned is named Elara. They are under strict instruction to only find and bring Elara back, and no one else.

"Tell me you're listening, both of you?" I snap, they whip their heads to me and nod.

"Please don't make me use my alpha command on you." It's one of the disadvantages of being an alpha, though some alphas would say it's one of the best parts; When you give an order in your alpha command, they must submit and obey it and couldn't defy even if they wanted to.

"Goddess, the first day in my new pack and I'm already getting an alpha warning," Lola mutters, rolling my eyes, but I ignore her.

"Kylo, please."

"You got it, Boss. Go, get ready for us back home, and we will be back a day after you, that's all. I'll call you on the way." His voice is gentle but the slap he gives on my back is anything but. I nod and watch until they disappear from the cave.

△△△

It's early in the morning when we arrive back at our pack lands with no word from Kylo. I can only hope he and Lola listened.

I pull up in my SUV outside our pack house and drop some of the men off, telling them to go rest. We can do a debrief and replan when Kylo returns. Popping the car back into drive, I head for my home. Although I have a room in the pack house, I also have my parents' cabin just outside of the main pack village. I could do without the questions from the elders and council, so I'll head there to rest up.

We are lucky to have such beautiful land. We do not need to go to the human towns or cities, as we grow our own fruits and veggies and have a farmer who provides the right meats, corn fields, and other supplies. Our schools educate the pups we have, and our health care centre has the up-to-date equipment it needs.

This time of day is my favourite when the sun is starting to rise above the skyline, and you can catch it as it hits the thatched roofs on the houses and shops. It's picturesque, aesthetically pleasing as Kylo would say.

Turning right off the main road, I head up the hills toward my family cabin. You can't reach it by car, and my dad preferred it this way. He would tell me, *"One day, you'll understand why I built the house like this, no surprise visits."* He was right, as usual... I really do understand it. Taking care of the pack is tiring, mentally draining, and there's days where you wish you could just switch off and take some me time, but you can't.

I pull into the drive my dad made at the top of one of the hills and get out, then close my eyes for a brief second to take in the silence around me.

*"Sleep. Bed. Sleep,"*Axel, my wolf, calls out to me.

Agreeing with him for once, I stroll through the woods and cross the bridge to home.

△△△

CHAPTER 7 – ELARA

The night of the mating ceremony

Fortunately, because of the mating ceremony, we make it out of holding cells without being seen, but unfortunately, we still have to make it across the pack lands and over the boarder without being sniffed out. Simple, right?

If I can just pick up Lola's scent, I can follow it.

I have no idea who took her, but this is Lola, she's a fighter, so if they were bad, well, goddess bless their souls. And any chance they are good people, she's probably fighting with them to come back, so she won't be far away.

Whispering "We can do this" to Jack and watching his beautiful little face light up. I come up with a plan. If I can make it to the medical centre, I can shift behind there and then Jack can get on my back, and I run it out the pack lands. I'll be quicker that way and less likely to be caught. And if any danger shows, well il figure it out in the moment.

As am I about to step out of the shadows, an explosion followed by screams comes from the town centre.

"Jack, look at me." His blue eyes are wide, and his mouth is agape. "Jack, I'm going to shift, and then you need to get on my back and hold on tight. Do. Not. Let. Go. No matter what, stay on my back, okay?" He nods, and I call forward my wolf as I haven't formally met her, yet I just plead in my mind for my wolf, by now I should have met her and know her name but for whatever reason she's not ready to meet me. I know she's there and can hear me because my bones start to snap although this shift hurts a little it's not as much as the first time.

When I feel its completed, I ask my wolf to lay down Jack gets on my back and grips my fur tightly, I beg my wolf to protect him. In a silent agreement from my wolf, we bound forward out of the shadows and across the pack lands weaving in and out of the cabins dotted about.

$$\triangle\triangle\triangle$$

CHAPTER 8 – LOLA

The night of the mating ceremony

Only I would meet my fated mate on the first day I fucking shift. We don't complete the mating until we have marked each other, so we cannot communicate through a mindlink yet, which is probably for the best, considering the douche bag infuriates the life out of me.

"Yeah, but a douche bag we love," my wolf, Zena, informs me.

"You're on my shit list too, Zen." I haven't figured out how to shut her out yet.

"Come on, Lola, look at his wolf." She drools and I gag, and I swear Knox, his wolf, winked at us.

However, no time for that yet. I have one thing on my mind: Get Elara out of there for good.

She thinks I'm fucking stupid, and I didn't know she was planning on leaving me. She didn't know I've had my bags packed and ready to go too.

When I met Kylo last night, I was coming in from my first run and could smell him as I crossed the border. With Zena screaming mate and the strength of his scent, I followed the trail. As soon as he came into view, I screamed for Elara, and in hindsight, that was an error.

I alerted the whole pack, but I saw it as our way out, as he looked big enough to help us. If the tales of fated mates are true, he can't say no to me.

Like I said, hindsight, and it's a wonderful thing, right?

Now I am trying to get back into the pack to save my best friend while keeping Zena from humping the leg of our new mate.

I thought about asking Alpha Asher what Elara being a white wolf means, but something stopped me. She was always different from everyone else, and this confirmed it. When we get back to our new pack lands, I will look it up, though Elara and I need to have that conversation first.

As I snap out of my thoughts when we reach the pack lines, I step in front of Knox to lead them in, but he headbutts me and gives a warning growl. *Fine. You lead the way; see how far you get before your tomorrow's special meal on the dinner menu.*

A loud bang goes off in the centre of the town, and I jump behind Knox. He shifts back into his human form and crouches in front of me. "Hey, Zena, ain't you beautiful?" She purrs, and I gag again. "Brock and Harvey are going to get a little closer to see what's going on, and we are gonna stay here until they give the all clear." He stares down at us for a beat, gently scratching Zena's head, then winks and shifts back.

CHAPTER 9 – KYLO

The night of the mating ceremony

This is easily the most scared I've ever been.

I've fought plenty of time in my life, and Knox is amazing is amazing in wolf form, but with my fated mate beside me, this is a whole new level of fear. We are outnumbered, with no backup plan. I did not think this through.

Probably should have listened to the bossman. If Asher were here, he'd be yelling that if I was ever an alpha, he'd invade me and take my pack and privileges away for being a fucking idiot.

Several more explosions go off, one after another, hitting various landmarks around the town. One caused Lola to shift back and attempt running toward the orphanage, which is now up in flames. I wasn't having any of it and stopped her. It broke my heart to see her crying for Elara, but she's my priority in life and it's not safe for her here. Calling Brock and Harvey back to us via mindlink after deciding enough was enough, we head back home to come up with a new plan.

Luckily for wolves in human or wolf form we are quick on our feet with Lola sobbing for me to help her friend and not wanting to risk her I shifted back into human form I picked up my mate, sprinting towards the direction of the vehicles staying in the tree lines while the others flanked either side of us.

△△△

CHAPTER 10 – ELARA

The night of the mating ceremony

T ears fill my eyes as the orphanage I once called home goes up in flames.

Jack taps my head and whispers for me to go. So, I do. Calling out to my wolf, I urge her to push harder and faster. With wolves fighting all around us, I knew we couldn't stay here. I have no training in my wolf form, and with her not talking to me, we are useless in a fight; we need to make it to the boarder, then we should be okay.

As I sprint through what was once our tattered town, I try to avoid being seen while weaving through dead bodies—wolf and human. I hoped my white fur would be misinterpreted because of the scorching flames bellowing out of shop windows, but wolves stop fighting to watch me pass by. I wanted to stop and ask what the big deal was with my fur, but I wanted out more. Maddox's wolf caught my attention as he darted for the tree line behind the medical centre. I can't let him see me. *Just keep pushing*.

"Where do you think you're heading, white wolf." Maddox's voice comes through my mindlink.

"Shut him out!" I scream at my wolf. Silence.

Jack screams, "Stop," and I know its Maddox through his mind link.

As I cross the border, I skid to a halt to try to spot Maddox; last thing I need is that asshole following us. My shoulders sting as Jack grips my fur and begs me to keep moving.

Maddox comes into view, we lock eyes, and then he drops to his paws and bows his head before yelling, *"Run, Elara, Run*!" in our mindlink. And I do.

I spin and bolt. For what or where, I don't know but I cry at my wolf to keep pushing us forward.

Why didn't Maddox chase after? And why would he try saving me by telling me to run?

△△△

I wake up hours later in human form with Jack nestled in under my arm.

The last thing I remember is coming into this cave after catching Lola's scent, but then a stronger scent masked hers in here. It's not unpleasant, but it's making it harder to find her.

"Hey, Jack Jack, you awake, sweet boy?" I whisper to him while stroking his hair out of his eyes.

"Mm," he murmurs while fluttering his eyes open. "I'm hungry."

Oh shit. We left in such a hurry and panic I didn't even think to grab supplies.

It's frequent practice to leave clothes, ration packs, and bottles of water in holes in the trees around the lands, especially outside of the pack borders, just in case you need to shift back into human form quickly. Although, most wolves are not afraid of being naked, I was thankful I found some women's clothes inside a tree last night.

Maybe if I go back out in the daylight, I might find us something to eat and drink. My stomach lets out a loud grumble, letting me know I am also hungry. *That's a definite yes to food.*

I kneel in front of him and place a hand on his cheek. "I will get you something along the way, for now we need to keep moving, okay? I'm not sure what happened last night, but the farther away we get, the better."

Jack gives me the sweetest lopsided smile and nods. "Okay, El, I can wait. Are we going to see Lola?"

My heart sinks. This must be so hard for him to understand, as he's only six years old. "I have her scent." It's a half-truth; I kind of have it. *If I follow this strong scent, maybe I can find her? Or not, but what other option do we have?*

I nod and grab his hand, gently pulling him along with me out of the cave. "We are going to find her."

ΔΔΔ

CHAPTER 11 – ALPHA ASHER

Kylo and Lola returned two days ago. I'd be lying if I said something hasn't shifted in the air. I've been racking my brain since then. Problem is, we are out of the loop, and because of that, I have no idea what threats lie ahead for us. Though, it's been this way since we were kicked out and it's not crossed my mind before.

"You're in overthinking mode, brother," Ella says, pulling me out my thoughts.

"How could you possibly know El, you're even not in the same room."

"That's correct; however, I can hear your huge flipper feet banging on the ceiling above me as you pace the length of your office floor." She huffs through the mindlink. *"Look, I don't think they suspect us to be the reason for the bombings at the Shadow Moon Pack. If the elders did, then we would know about it by now."*

True, she has a point. They wouldn't waste any time showing up here if that was the case. *Wait!*

"Would you stop reading my thoughts!" I snap.

"I'm going to take that as an agreement with me." Then she cuts off our link.

Every damn time. She's in my head. Ella isn't like most wolves. She's a hybrid—part human, part wolf, and part witch. Our mother was the same. It was passed down through genetics, as our Grandfather Turin was fated to a witch named Sybil. He and her were what the elders of our pack called a rarity. It was frowned upon by a lot of the pack members, mostly out of fear mom would tell us. A fear of what the two of them could do or create but they were crazy about one another. *True fated mates.*

So, when they started a family and had Mom, she was gifted with the ability to shift and use magic. It made growing up in our home fun. Mom would cast her spells around the home for cleaning or cooking, or if dad pissed her off, she'd zap him in the ass with an electric-shock spell.

Naturally, my parents assumed I'd have that ability too, but I never did. They figured it was because the alpha gene I inherited from my father overpowered it. They thought after having me they could only make

63

normal pups until she came along, but they never told me about Ella's powers. I figured it out the night she woke me up about the attack on our lands.

She finally cracked and told me, explaining that our parents thought it best to keep it to only those who needed to know, as there were too many dangers out there if word spread to other packs about Ella being a hybrid. They were worried I would slip up and tell someone like Kylo, who might tell someone else, and so on. She explained it's why we only ever saw Mom do spells inside the house. She kept it to a minimum outside of our home. *For the safety of us.*

"Bossman," Kylo shouts right before my office door swings open. His hair has fallen from its manbun, and he's soaked in sweat and. ... lipstick? *Yep, just stopped fucking Lola to come here.* I raise my brow, and he nods, then sucks in a deep breath before he says, "Come quick; we got visitors."

$$\triangle\triangle\triangle$$

Ella's in the doorway when I reach the bottom of the stairs, and when she spins around, her face is pale, her eyes wide, and brows knitted together. Stopping in my tracks, I tilt my head. "Ella, what is it?"

"Wolves but not from our pack, a girl and boy," she whispers, then looks back over her shoulder toward our pack border.

"Rogues?" I question.

Shaking her head from side to side, she answers, "I'm not sure, I don't think so."

I take a few steps toward her and pull her in for a hug. "Okay, stay inside. Kylo and I will check it out." I kiss her head and let her go, but she grabs my hand.

"Do you have to go?" she whispers as tears well in her eyes, and I know why; these are people she doesn't know, and since we only have each other left, she's terrified something will happen to me, the same way I am with her.

"Ella, this is part of my job. It's my responsibility to investigate who is out there." Trying to keep my voice level while blocking her from my mind is a tricky thing to do, but it stops her from invading my thoughts and seeing I get as worried as she does.

Letting her go again, I walk out of the pack house toward to border hut. "Let's see who the fuck wants in, shall we?" I say to Kylo as we pick up our pace into a sprint.

△△△

CHAPTER 12 – ELARA

W e've been on the run for two days, and though it's been hard to keep alert and keep track of Lola's scent, I think I'm in the right place. I hope? Only thing is I have no clue where we are or who took her.

I place Jack in an abandoned cabin, arming him with a bat I found in a cupboard, and tell him to stay put until I return, and if anything happens to me, I told him to run in the opposite direction.

Taking a deep breath, I close the door and make my way toward the unknown pack border lines. I spotted a few wolves shifting last night when we were studying the lands, and something in my gut told me that's where we need to head. *I will not shift*, I tell myself. *I don't want to be a threat.*

"Hi, my name's Elara, I was previously a member of the Shadow Shifters Pack, and I have reason to believe my best friend is here." *No, that's too much.* Maybe I don't mention the Shadow Shifters Pack. That might put me in a bad light, considering the place was burning to the ground when we fled.

"Hi, my name is Elara, I think you have my sister." *Yes, sister.* That's more likely to get me the answers I need, but it's still not perfect.

"Hi, I'm Elara, and I was tortured and beaten by my last pack. I've been travelling for days, and I need sleep and someone to take a six-year-old off my hands. Also, do you have my sister, Lola?"

Jack and I were lucky that we didn't cross any rogues or stumble into other packs, but we are starving and thirsty. And I could seriously do with seeing Lola so she can take Jack and watch him while I rest.

Breathe, Elara, you can do this.

"Halt!" A deep voice shouts from ahead of me. I had been too busy watching my feet squelch in the mud to pay attention to where I was going. Stopping in my tracks, I keep my head bowed.

Something stirs inside of me, and my eyes flutter. *Fuck, something smells good.*

At this point, I don't care what happens. I'd use my dying wish to get to that scent. *Do you think they'd grant it?*

"State your name and your business." His voice is smooth but gruff at the same time, and I hum in response. I have no idea what's wrong with me, but my stomach is exploding with butterflies, and my head's blank.

A voice from within screams, "*Mate!*" over and over again. My body heats up, and I'm desperate to take my clothes off. Luckily, a small part of my brain is keeping me together. *"Mate!"*

"Goddess, would you stop screaming," I say aloud. I close my eyes and drop to my knees and whisper, "What the fuck is wrong with me?"

"Are you okay?" It's a different the voice this time, and I still don't look up but tilt my head in the direction footsteps are coming from. Then a growl roars around me, and it rocks my core, tightening every muscle in my body.

"Get away from my mate, now!" The first voice I heard booms followed gasps from whoever is around me. I'd love to look up, but my head is almost too heavy with air to hold upright.

"*Mate, our mate!*" the voice inside my head shouts again.

I'm about to ask this voice what the fuck it's talking about when Jack cries out, "Get away from my mommy." I snap back into reality and jump up and spin to Jack running to me. As he gets closer, a loud growl sounds are us, and it sends shivers down my spine, then the smell invades my nose again. This time, I feel a breath on my shoulder from behind me.

"Mate," I whisper.

△△△

CHAPTER 13 – ALPHA ASHER

Running over to the border hut, I had to stop to control Axel, as he was flipping out and screaming, "Mate!" over and over. Kylo could sense something was wrong.

"You good, Bossman?" He places a hand on my shoulder, and I look down at him.

"Yeah, yeah, just Axel, I can't shut him up," I say, rubbing the back of my neck.

"What's up with him?" Kylo asks, his brows furrowed.

"Doesn't matter. Let's go." I don't wait for him to reply and pick my pace up. Hair's sprout along my arms, and I shout to Axel,"*What the fuck is going on with you, I'm not letting you out not until you've calmed down.*"

"*Mate, mine*," he growls back. My whip my head to one side hoping to catch him off guard. Last thing I need right now is my wolf pushing through when he's like this.

I come to a group of my warriors when the smell id picked up a few moments go hits me hard and it's driving Axel wild.

I push through them as Harvey comes into view. I can feel Axel pushing harder against me he lets out a warning growl to Harvey who immediately drops his head to bow. *"Axel, stop!"*

I look back at Kylo, mindlinking him to tell Harvey, "*It's Axel with the problem, not me, tell him not to worry.*"

As I get to the front of the crowd, a slim brunette is walking toward us, and everything snaps into place. This is my mate. She's breathtaking, even though she's awfully thin and has cuts covering her arms and legs. *Look at me.*

Why hasn't she healed herself? Wolves heal quickly, so those cuts on her arms and legs should have disappeared in minutes.

"Halt!" The word comes out harsh, and guilt eats at me for speaking to my mate like that, but *look at me, damn it.*

She stops, then sniffs the air, and Axel jumps in excitement while shouting, "*She wants us too.*"

Her voice comes out like silk as she speaks. "Goddess, would you stop screaming." I almost launch for her when she falls to the ground. A million questions flying around my brain.

What's her name?

Where has she come from?

Why is she hurt? I mindlink Trevor, the pack doctor, to come check her over at the pack house.

Kylo comes up beside me. *"How's Axel holding up?"* He winks and smirks before walking toward my mate and asking her, "Are you okay?"

Axel roars, "Get away from my mate, now!"

My warriors gasp and bow while Kylo laughs.

"Knew it, welcome to the love club, brother."

"Fuck off and don't ever get close to her again." I shut him out.

Taking slow steps toward her, a small kid comes running up the dirt track. Before I order him to stop, he screams, "Get away from my mommy." She jumps up and turns to face him.

Axel growls, and I can't say I disagree with him this time.

Who the fuck got my mate pregnant?

△△△

"Jack, it's okay, sweet boy." Jack runs into her arms.

Jealously rips through me and a growl escapes that I didn't want to let out.

She whirls around in my direction and looks me in the eyes for the first time. Her dark-chocolate gaze bores into me, and she opens her mouth slightly. Her fangs have dropped down, and Axel gets excited again, claiming, "*She wants to mark us, let her.*"

"*She's ready to fight us if you growl at her kid again,*" I tell him.

She takes a step back from me, and I feel a pang of loss. *She doesn't want us. She's going to reject us. Is it the pup's dad? Is he why she doesn't want us?*

Like she can hear my thoughts, she says, "I'm scared since you haven't gotten Axel under control and worried, you're going to hurt Jack. Being my mate doesn't mean you get to decide who is in my life." Her voice is still the sweetest thing I've ever heard, even if she is upset with me.

"How do you know about Axel?"

"I just met my wolf, literally right before you shouted halt. And apparently, she's able to connect with Axel, and she told him to calm down around Jack because you're both scaring him."

My emotions are in overdrive. Whatever my mate's wolf said to Axel worked, as he has blocked me out completely.

"I think he got the message; do you want to come into the pack house, eh, for food, water, rest…" I rub the back of my neck.

Her eyes well up with unshed tears, and she bites her bottom lip.

"*This is a lot for her too, Ash.*" Ella's voice comes through our mindlink. "By the looks of it, she's had a rough time. And right now, she's a mom protecting her pup. You need to go hug her; that will snap the bond into place, and she will see you're not that fucking scary." Looking away from my mate and her pup, I spot Ella next to a tree.

"Everyone go back to work; you treat my mate and her pup like one of us going forward, got it?" My tone is harsh, but I want to make sure the message is driven home. Not that I needed to; this will be a celebration for our pack. I don't give anyone time to respond before I shut off the link to them all.

"My name's Elara Devlin, and this little pup is Jack Quinn." She smiles at him. "Well, we are both orphans. My parents died in a car crash, and no one knows much about Jack's life before he joined us. I've just turned eighteen and Jack's six." Her voice is shaky, and a few tears fall down her cheek.

Then she breaks my heart. "I understand if you want to reject me as your luna. I know omegas, especially orphaned ones, are not thought of as much in the packs, if not at all, so I understand if you don't want me. If you do, for whatever crazy reason, want me, I need you to know Jack is not my pup by blood, but he is like my pup. I couldn't leave him in that pack, and I won't send him back, we are a package deal." *She thinks I'm going to reject her? Goddess, what happened to her back at her pack?*

She cries into Jack's shoulder, and his little arms wrap around her neck. I step forward and pull them both into my arms. They freeze for a second before relaxing into me.

"What was the pack you both come from," I whisper.

"Shadow Shifters Pack, Alpha," Jack answers, and I smile at him. *Sweet kid.*

Elara, my mate's name is Elara, and they are from the pack Lola was in.

"I have someone I think you both might want to see."

△△△

CHAPTER 14 – ELARA

The moment those words leave his beautiful lips, I know he's talking about Lola.

I gasp. "She's here?"

He nods. "Yeah, she's here, she and her mate, my beta, went back to the pack to find you, but it was too dangerous to stay, so Kylo brought her here. She's been pissed with him since."

I laugh. "Sounds like Lola." I smile and wipe my tears.

"I'm hungry," Jack whispers in my ear. I look up at my mate, and from the smile on his face, he heard Jack.

He points toward a large building in the distance. "Jack, I can carry you if you like? We can go get some food for you and your mom. She looks tired, don't you think?" If my heart could have burst in that moment, it would have. I meant every word I said to him. Jack and I are a package deal. I won't ever leave him alone. The fact he is addressing me to Jack as his mom makes me happy.

"Elara!" Lola screams, and my heartrate picks up, and Jack squeals while he jumps out of my arms and sprints to Lola. I smile at my mate and follow Jack.

"Hey, pup." Lola laughs as she picks Jack up and squeezes him.

I dive into her, sandwiching Jack between us. "Oh, Lola." I sob into her shoulder, and she cries with me. "We missed you so much," I tell her.

"I missed you more."

The three of us hold each other for what feels like forever, and part of me wants to bottle this moment up and stay here forever, but my mate clears his throat, interrupting us.

"Asher," Lola grits out. *So that's my mate's name.*

"Elara and Jack are hungry and tired. Why don't we take them inside?" he asks, but his tone says this is not up for debate. I look behind Lola to see a tall, broad man with a man bun on the top of his head.

Smiling, he steps forward. "Kylo." He holds his hand out for me to shake, and Asher growls.

Kylo throws his hands up in the air. "Come the fuck on, Ash, she's about to be our new luna, get used to people being around your mate." I let out a giggle.

"Shut the hell up, you guys are mates? Like fated mates, mates?" Lola asks, her eyes wide and mouth in a perfect o shape. My cheeks are burning, so I dip my head slightly, so Asher doesn't see, and nod.

Fated mates.

△△△

As I get out of the shower, there is a knock on the door. Too tired to deal with people, I ignore it.

After finally seeing Lola, we had a lot to catch up on. So, the five of us: Lola, Jack, Kylo, Asher, and I all sat down to eat dinner, and I told them everything that happened after I shifted for the first time. Lola always got angry when I told her what Maddox did to me, but it was weird for me to have Asher and Kylo angry too. I guess I'm just not used to having people care.

"That's a lot to unpack," Kylo says with a mouthful of food. "So, let me get this straight, you're a white-furred wolf?"

Lola snorts. "That's the part you picked up on?" And she points her fork at Kylo's nose.

Jack covers his ears with his hands. "Oh no, now you're in trouble, Ky," he tells him. Asher and I laugh.

The look on Kylo's face says he also knows he's in the wolf house.

Asher's sat beside me, and his eyes are glazed over; he is mindlinking someone. I shouldn't be jealous, he's an alpha, he will be linking people all day, every day. Like he can see the thoughts running through my mind, he leans down and kisses the top of my head.

As Lola lays into Kylo and Jack giggles at them, Asher asks me to join him on a walk, and once outside and out of earshot, he tells me, "I've got Jack a room sorted. It is opposite our room, but I completely understand if you would rather, he sleeps next to you for now. I can go into another room." He wrings his hands out in front of him and avoids eye contact with me.

"Can we go to the bedroom?" I pause, thinking that might sound inappropriate, like I'm offering him something I'm not ready for. "Jack's new room, I'd like to see it, please," I add, hoping to clear up what I meant.

He nods and smiles; then points in the direction he wants to take me. "Sure."

We make our way from the cook house to the pack house in comfortable silence. I'm not sure what's going to happen, what my future holds here, but it feels good to know I have Lola, Jack, and now Asher and Kylo with me. I know I am nowhere near ready to be Luna. I wonder if maybe Asher's mom can show me the ropes? She would have been the old luna, she would know what to do.

As we get to the stairs at the front of the pack house, Asher grabs my hand, interlocking our fingers. "Sorry, I can let go if you like." His cheeks burn red, and I shake my head from side to side.

"No, don't, it's okay."

I like it.

△△△

The knock on my door sounds again. *Ugh!*

"Just a minute," I call out.

My whole-body aches as I put the clothes on Asher left out for me.

I open my bedroom door to a petite white-haired, girl and her eyes are closed as she looks at her feet. Touching her shoulder, I ask, "Are you okay?" Her eyes flick open, and I jump back. *She has purple eyes. Purple eyes?!*

"I'm so sorry. You gave me quite the fright." I try to regain my composure.

"Sorry, I have that effect on most people." She gives a small smile. "I know you didn't want to be interrupted; I can see you're tired, but I just wanted to introduce myself."

"It's okay, no problem. I'm Elara Devlin." I hold out my hand for her to shake, and she does, then lets out a cute giggle.

"Oh, I know who you are, if I didn't, I think my big brother would not be happy. I'm Ella, Alpha Asher's sister."

He has a sister?

"Yes, he does," she answers like she can read my mind. "You guys haven't had much time to yourselves, which is the other reason I'm here. I've come to offer my babysitting services. I'd love to get to know my new nephew, Jack, and you need time with your mate." She rocks back and forth on her heels with her hands clasped in front of her.

I give her a smile. "I'd love that, Ella." She beams, and her purple eyes shine.

"Thank you," I tell her.

CHAPTER 15 – ALPHA ASHER

I wake up with the sun beaming through my windows after enjoying what I know was the best night's sleep I've ever had. Elara is cuddled into me, her back against my chest and head on my arm, sleeping soundly.

The urge to mark her neck and claim her as my luna and the need to kiss her lips is strong, but I can't, not until she's ready to. I want her to come to me willingly. She's had way too many people from her old pack take from her, by the sounds of it, without her consent.

If I could, I'd burn that pack to the ground. I will.

I slowly move out from behind her, not that I want to but duty calls. I have a lot I need to get done this morning. I'm thinking of taking Elara and Jack to my family house in the hills for the night.

"Already planned it, brother."

Damn it, Ella. I groan, waking Elara.

"How many time have I got to tell you. Stay. Out. Of. My. Head."

"Chill out. I'm going to look after Jack. Don't worry, I got her blessing to babysit him last night, aaaaand before you say shit, if I struggle, Lola has me covered. Kylo has the pack covered. And you're taking Elara to the house. Yoooooou're welcome." She sings the last part out, and then shuts off the mindlink.

I sit on the bed, placing my elbows on my knees and my head in my hands, taking deep breaths in through my nose and blowing them out through my mouth.

I'm happy to have some alone time with Elara, but is she okay with it? She might have been so tired last night she didn't know what she was saying, or she did and just said yes to be polite.

"Are you okay?" Her sweet voice calms me as she strokes my back.

"Yeah," I say, debating on whether I tell her, so I throw caution to the wind and go for it. "Ella has planned some time away for us, just us." I pause and lie back to face her. "It's okay if you don't want to, you know, just say the word."

82

"No, I think it will be nice for us." She smiles, and I return it. "I don't know anything about you, and I want to." her cheeks flame up at her admission, and Axel stirs. "*Ask her to run with me*!"he shouts.

"Axel is desperate for me to shift, right? Emma, my wolf, told me he doesn't shut up about it." She winks and I laugh.

No surprise there. "You and Emma getting along, then." I push a loose strand of her hair behind her ear.

"Yeah, I think so, she didn't show up right away like Zena did for Lola. It took you to bring her out. She still won't tell me why though." Her bottom lip pops out, and she bites it, furrowing her brows.

"Mm, maybe it's what happened at your last pack. Maybe she blocked herself away until she felt safe again? We can call Doctor Trevor back to see if he knows why? He might be able to run some tests and find out why she hid?"

I got Doctor Trevor to check over Elara and Jack last night. They are a little malnourished for wolves, but I needed to know everything else was okay.

He told me Elara had broken bones in the past that never healed properly. Before you get your wolf at eighteen, you need a doctor to mend you properly. After eighteen your wolf does that for you. So, with Elara being beaten by those assholes and not taken to a doctor, her bones didn't heal correctly.

"No, it's okay, I don't want the fuss, but I'm ready to get out of here the moment you are." She rolls out of bed and runs to the bathroom.

She's fucking perfect.

△△△

"It's quite the bachelor pad you have here," Elara declares as she looks around.

I smirk and cross my arms over my chest. "Mm, hardly, it's my home. Just needs a woman's touch to it is all." I wink at her when she spins around to face me.

With cheeks stained red, in a voice just above a whisper she asks, "Aaand are you looking for a woman?"

I stroll over to her with every bit of confidence I can muster, curl my pointer finger under her chin, and lift her head up to look at me. "No, baby, I'm looking at my woman."

Elara's eyelids flutter shut, and she whispers, "Kiss me, Asher."

Finally. I lower my lips onto hers, softly kissing her, and goose bumps scatter across my arms as she curls her hand around my neck to pull me closer. Our gentle kiss turns primal, then our tongues dance and teeth clash. When she bites and pulls my lower lip with her teeth, though I'm done for.

Moaning into each other's mouths, I can smell her arousal. Her tight little cunt is begging to be touch, licked, sucked, and fucked by me, and baby, am I happy to deliver.

I pull away from her kiss, wanting to touch every part of her body, and lick space between her neck and shoulder, where she'll one day sport my mark, all the way up to her jawline. "How wet are you for me, El?"

She's shudders beneath me before pulling her dress over her head.

She stands in front of me in a lilac lace thong and bra. "Find the fuck out, Asher. Touch me here." She points to her pussy, and I pounce like a man starved.

My claws extend from my fingers, and I swipe the thongs off her body, moaning instantly when my hand slides between her folds and her pussy soaks my fingers. "As much as I want to take my time with you, I need to fuck right now, do you think you're ready, El?" My voice is husky, and I nip her neck over I slip my fingers in and out of her.

She's close to coming all over my hand. "Ahh, just do it," she rasps out.

Ripping my trousers off in one swift motion, I slide my hand to her perfect ass and lift her up before slamming her down onto my straining cock. "Asher, fuck, yes," she screams. "More."

Pounding into her, she cries out as she reaches climax. I chase it with my own and slip over the edge with her, calling her name out as I empty my seed into her.

△△△

The last three weeks have flown by, and Elara is warming up to becoming my luna. We've not marked each other yet, but I'm ready to, and I think she is as well.

Today we have a meeting with the pack elders to discuss Elara's Luna ceremony and to probe about her white wolf situation. After failing to find anything in the pack library about a white wolf, they are the only ones who might possibly know what it means. Elara agreed with me that its best until we have answers that she doesn't shift.

Jack is warming to Axel. I've shifted a few times so Jack could pet him and see he's not scary. Axel adores him, as do I, and he's got himself a little friend from school named Benji.

Lola has Kylo completely by the balls. Better still, the pack adores all three of our new members. Life's fucking great. What more could I want.

Or, at least, it was until Harvey came barrelling into my office.

"Alpha, come quick, Alpha Maddox is at the front gate, and er, he's demanding to see Luna Elara."

Alpha Maddox?! What happened to Alpha Blake, and what the fuck does he want with my woman?

TO BE CONTINUED....

ACKNOWLEDGMENTS

Truthfully, this book was supposed a lot longer and as a duet, not a trilogy.

Buuuut I got serious burnout while writing this and another book side by side and then planning both releases in the span of a month… alongside my main work and family life.

I know some of you have been waiting for this book to come out after reading *Yours Truly*, and I hate to be a disappointment, so I hope you liked this snippet I've written.

This story took over my life. It's woken me up and kept me up at night, stumbled in during work meetings, and consumed me during times of sitting on the toilet at home.

What this book taught me was I can't write two books at once in two genres ha-ha. Jokes aside, this book ignited my love for paranormal romance.
I can confidently say we won't leave this world any time soon.

So, books 2 and 3 are coming in 2024. I know you will have a lot of questions about this book already but don't fret all will be answered in the next two **and both will be full length!!!**

There will be other series set in the same world as this but for other characters in this book. I'm setting a timeframe for 2025 for this.

As always, I adore every single one of you.
Thank you to every reader and reviewer. You're all besties to me. Your support is so kind and means everything.
To family and friends, thanks for dealing with me while I was a jerk and wrote this; I'm sorry for the way I acted.

Until the next time,

Laura
Xoxo

ABOUT THE AUTHOR LAURA RUSH

Laura Rush is 30 years old and released her debut
novel *Yours Truly* in June 2023.
She lives in North Yorkshire, UK with her
husband, son, and dog.
Laura writes Rom-Com romances with a hella load
of smut.

She enjoys martinis, long walks, and reading.

Find her on socials:
Instagram - @authorlaurarush
Facebook - @authorlaurarush
TikTok - @authorlaurarush

Website and newsletter coming soon!

Printed in Great Britain
by Amazon

36777410R00056